Braelen

Treat others as you would

like to be treated.

Dana Lehman

W9-BRT-952

Adventures at Walnut Grove

A Lesson about Teasing

Written by Dana Lehman • Illustrations by Judy Lehman

Lehman
Publishing
ALLENTON, MICHIGAN

Copyright © 2007 by Dana Lehman
Second Edition

All rights reserved. No part of this publication may be reproduced or stored
in a retrieval system or transmitted in any form or by any means,
electronic, mechanical, photocopying, recording, or otherwise,
without the prior written permission of the publisher.
Printed and bound in Hong Kong

Published by Lehman Publishing
15997 Hough Road
Allenton, Michigan 48002
www.lehmanpublishing.com

Edited by Imogene Zimmermann & Tina Hall
Design Layout by Gayle Brohl

Library of Congress Control Number: 2007901161

ISBN-13: 978-0-9792686-0-1
ISBN-10: 0-9792686-0-5

Acknowledgements

I would like to thank my mom, who told me squirrel stories when I was young. There was always a lesson behind every story, and I will never forget them. I would also like to thank my mother-in-law, Judy, for all her hard work and dedication. You brought the story to life beautifully. I also want to thank my husband, Brian, and our two sons Danny and Joey. They all gave me the courage and support to follow my dreams.

Dana Lehman

I have done various forms of art including oils, water colors and porcelain painting for thirty-five years. I am honored to illustrate this book for my daughter-in-law and grandsons.

Judy Lehman

Sammy was a unique squirrel.
Sammy had something
that no other animals in the forest had ever seen,
and that made him special.

Can you see what was different about Sammy?
He was a squirrel, but he had eyes like a raccoon.
He was different from all of the other squirrels,
but that didn't bother him.
Sammy had lots of friends,
and they all loved him just the way he was.
But it wasn't always that way…

School was out. Every summer Sammy and his family
went to Paradise Pond to stay at the Walnut Grove Resort.
What made this trip even more fun was that his friends,
Rocky, a raccoon, and Pokey, a porcupine, would be there.
They always had fun playing together.

There were many games to play;
one of their favorites was walnut ball.
Playing walnut ball was always exciting.
Every summer new animals came to the Walnut Grove Resort.
Sammy and his friends were excited to meet them.

It was time
for the first game
of the summer.
The teams were picked,
and Rocky was up to bat.
The first walnut was thrown
and Rocky hit a home run.
All of the animals cheered.
Rocky was one of the best
players on the team.
Sammy was up to bat next.
He wasn't as good a player
as his friend Rocky,
but he always tried his best,
and that was all that mattered.

Sammy was very nervous.
"Keep your eye on the walnut,
Sammy,"
yelled his Mommy.
"Hit a home run, Sammy!
You can do it!"
screamed his sister.

Sammy was about
to hit the walnut
when he heard something
that surprised him.

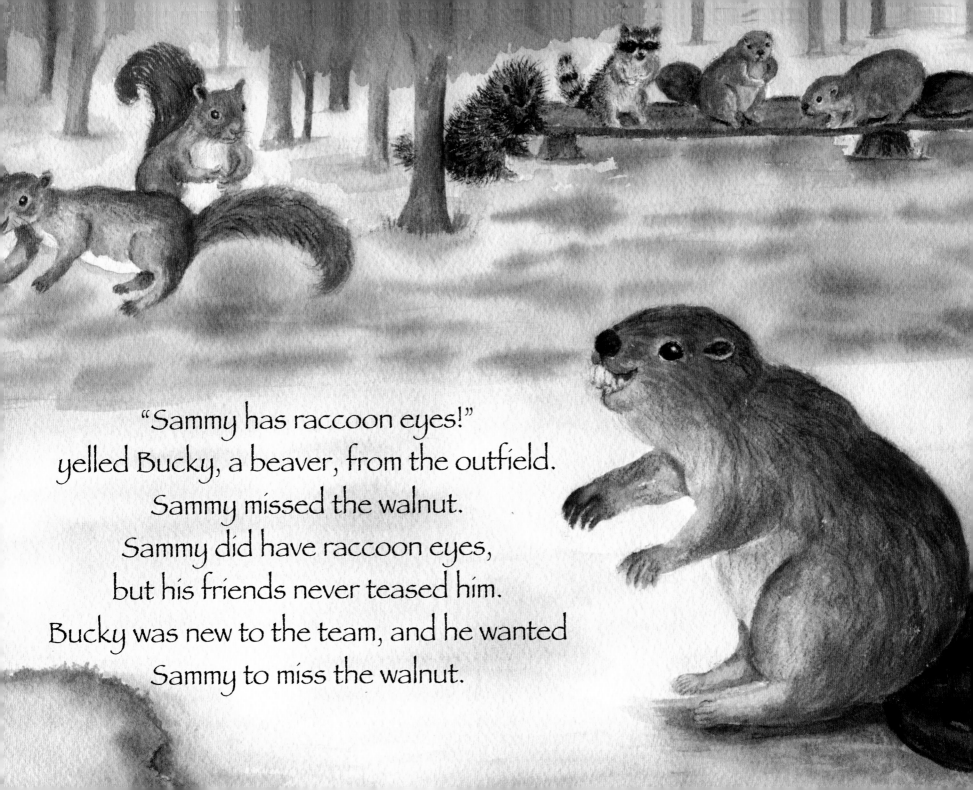

"Sammy has raccoon eyes!"
yelled Bucky, a beaver, from the outfield.
Sammy missed the walnut.
Sammy did have raccoon eyes,
but his friends never teased him.
Bucky was new to the team, and he wanted
Sammy to miss the walnut.

Sammy's feelings were hurt.

He never called animals in the forest bad names.

Sammy's mommy always told him to treat others
as he would like to be treated, and Sammy did just that.

He was always nice to other animals.

Sammy didn't understand why Bucky was teasing him.

He tried to ignore him,
but Bucky kept right on calling him raccoon eyes.

Sammy struck out.

He couldn't get those words out of his head.

That afternoon, after the game,
all the animals went to Paradise Pond to go swimming.
Even though Bucky was a beaver,
he was not a very good swimmer.
All the animals knew that it was important
for a beaver to be a good swimmer, and so did Bucky.
He practiced every day and was getting better,
but his friends swam better than he did.

Pokey decided that swimming races would be fun,
and all the animals agreed, so they picked teams.
The problem was that no one wanted Bucky on his team.
He was picked last because he was a slow swimmer.
"Sorry you were picked last Bucky,
but you are a slow poke," said Pokey.

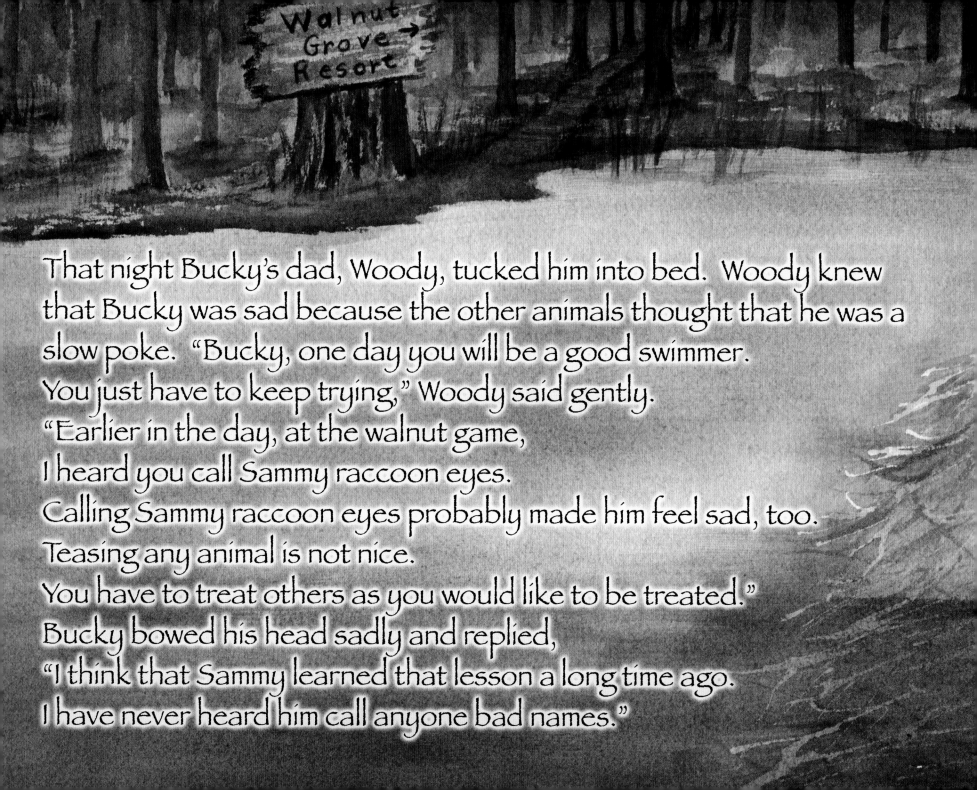

That night Bucky's dad, Woody, tucked him into bed. Woody knew
that Bucky was sad because the other animals thought that he was a
slow poke. "Bucky, one day you will be a good swimmer.
You just have to keep trying," Woody said gently.
"Earlier in the day, at the walnut game,
I heard you call Sammy raccoon eyes.
Calling Sammy raccoon eyes probably made him feel sad, too.
Teasing any animal is not nice.
You have to treat others as you would like to be treated."
Bucky bowed his head sadly and replied,
"I think that Sammy learned that lesson a long time ago.
I have never heard him call anyone bad names."

The next morning, as Bucky was walking to the field,
his mind drifted back to the swimming races at Paradise Pond.
Bucky recalled how upset he had been that he was called a slow poke.
Until that day at the pond,
he hadn't realized how wrong name-calling was.

Bucky approached the field and saw everyone practicing for the game.
He ran over to apologize to Sammy before the game started.
"Sammy, I am sorry for calling you raccoon eyes.
I was just trying to distract you
so that you wouldn't be able to hit the walnut.
I just wanted to win the game.
I didn't realize that I was hurting your feelings."

"I accept your apology, Bucky.
I hope that you will not call anyone bad names anymore,"
Sammy replied.
Bucky added, "I promise I won't do it again.
Now I know how it feels to be teased."

Pokey overheard them talking
and knew that he needed to apologize, too.
Pokey approached Bucky and said,
"I am sorry for calling you a slow poke;
it was not a very nice thing to say. I know that you
try your best when you swim and that's all that matters."
Bucky gave Pokey's words a lot of thought and then replied,
"I think we can all agree that
we will not be teasing anyone anymore."

That day they all had fun playing walnut ball.
No one teased anyone,
and no one worried about winning or losing.

They were just good friends,
having a good time, playing a game they loved.

How do you think Sammy felt when Bucky called him raccoon eyes?

What do you think you would say to make Sammy feel better
after Bucky called him raccoon eyes?

How do you think Bucky felt when he was picked last
for the swimming races?

How do you think Bucky felt when he was called a slow poke?

How do you think you would feel if someone called you a bad name?

What are some things you could do to help someone
who is being teased?

What are some things that you can do to get better at playing a game or sport?

A Word from the Author

Everyone looks different; that's what makes each of us unique. We have to appreciate people for who they are. It doesn't matter what you look like on the outside; what matters is who you are on the inside.
Everyone also has different physical abilities. No matter what you do in life you have to do things to the best of your ability. Remember, the more you practice the better you will get.

Please remember to treat other people the way that you would like to be treated. If you wouldn't like being called names please don't call other people names. It does not feel good to be teased.
It is not nice to tease anyone for the way they look or for what they do.

Adventures at Walnut Grove: A Lesson about Teasing is the first book in the Walnut Grove Series of children's books. Adventures at Walnut Grove is a silver recipient of the Mom's Choice Award for values and life lessons. All books in this series support character education. The second book in this series, I DOUBLE Dare You!, tackles the issue of peer pressure and being responsible for one's own actions. I DOUBLE Dare You! is also a silver recipient of the Mom's Choice Award for developing social skills.

The third book in this series, I CAN DO IT, helps children realize that with confidence, persistence and determination, they can achieve their goals. The fourth book in the Walnut Grove series, Remember When... is a story about the importance of friendship and compassion.

Dana resides in Allenton, Michigan, with her husband and their two children. Her children and love of nature continually inspire her to keep writing children's books.

Dana's mother-in-law, Judy Lehman, is her illustrator. Judy Lehman has been an artist and teacher for over forty years; she is a retired elementary school teacher. She currently resides in Hubbard Lake, Michigan, with her husband.

For more information on these books, including free lesson plans, please visit www.lehmanpublishing.com